EMMET TO THE RESCUE

by Julia March

DK
Penguin
Random
House

Senior Editor Tori Kosara
Senior Designer Anna Formanek
Designer Sam Bartlett
Design Assistant James McKeag
Pre-production Producer Marc Staples
Producer Louise Daly
Managing Editor Paula Regan
Managing Art Editor Jo Connor
Publisher Julie Ferris
Art Director Lisa Lanzarini
Publishing Director Simon Beecroft

Dorling Kindersley would like to thank Randi Sørensen,
Heidi K. Jensen, Paul Hansford, and Martin Leighton Lindhardt
at the LEGO Group.

Published in Great Britain in 2019 by
Dorling Kindersley Limited
80 Strand, London WC2R 0RL
A Penguin Random House Company

10 9 8 7 6 5 4 3 2 1
001–312560–Jan/2019

Page design copyright ©2019 Dorling Kindersley Limited

A CIP catalogue record for this book is available from the British Library.

ISBN: 978-0-24136-047-7

Printed and bound in China

www.dk.com
www.LEGO.com

A WORLD OF IDEAS:
SEE ALL THERE IS TO KNOW

Contents

Emmet

Emmet is a cheerful guy.
He rides a special bike.
Emmet lives in a city.

Aliens attack

Emmet has five good friends.
They are Lucy, Unikitty, Benny,
Metalbeard and Batman.
Oh no!
Aliens come from space.
They attack the city.

Benny

Metalbeard

Lucy

Unikitty

Batman

Sweet Mayhem

Sweet Mayhem is a space pilot.
She kidnaps Emmet's friends.
They fly away in her spaceship.

Space rescue

Emmet wants to rescue
his friends.
He builds his own spaceship.
Then he flies into space to
look for them.

Emmet's friends

Rex

Rex is a space pilot.
He sees that Emmet
is in danger.
Will Rex save Emmet?

Emmet and Rex

Rex's spaceship

Rex has a spaceship.
It looks like a big fist.
The ship has a crew
of dinosaurs.

The crew

The dinosaurs help Rex
on his spaceship.
They are always busy.

The dinosaurs are
ready for danger.
This one has two
laser cannons.

The dinosaurs
take breaks.
They drink coffee.

This dinosaur has wings.
He can fly.

The dinosaurs love
to skateboard.
It is fun!

New friends

Rex saves Emmet from danger.
Emmet likes Rex.

Teamwork

Emmet looks for his friends with Rex.

They are ready for an adventure!

Quiz

1. Where does Emmet live?

2. Who kidnaps Emmet's friends?

3. Who does Emmet want to find?

4. What do the dinosaurs love to do?

5. What looks like a big fist?

6. Who saves Emmet from danger?

Index